THIS BOOK
BELONGS TO:

Tiago Rafael Barahona

from Grandpa
Grandma Krabill

Christmas
2012

Day Is Done

by **PETER YARROW**

illustrated by **MELISSA SWEET**

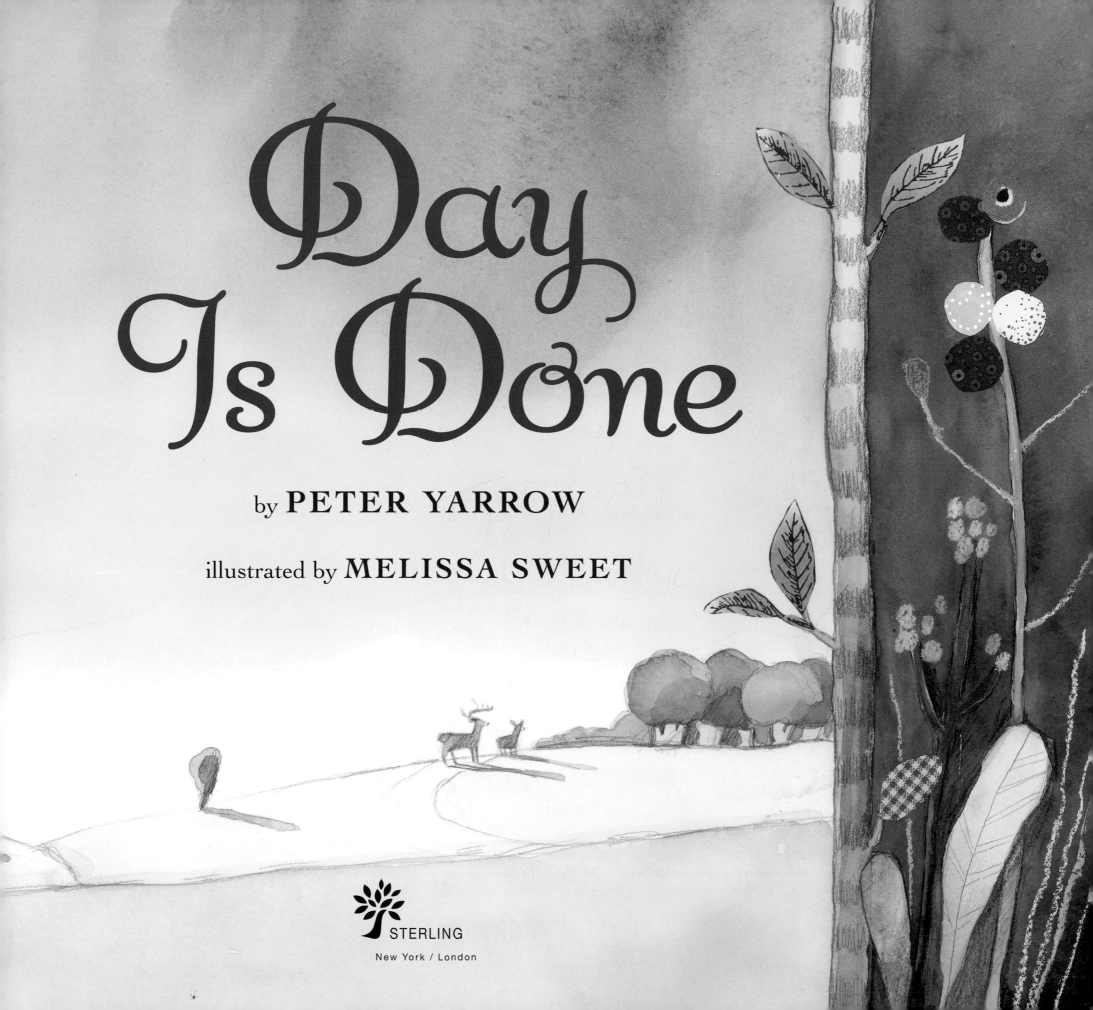

STERLING

New York / London

Tell me why you're crying, my son,
I know you're frightened, like everyone.

Is it the thunder in the distance you fear?
Will it help if I stay very near?

I am here.

And if you take my hand, my son,
All will be well when the day is done.

And if you take my hand, my son,
All will be well when the day is done.

Day is done, when the day is done.

When the day is done,
when the day is done.

Do you ask why I'm sighing, my son?

You shall inherit what humankind has done.

In a world filled with sorrow and woe,
If you ask me why, why is this so?

I really don't know.

But if you take my hand, my son,
All will be well when the day is done.

And if you take my hand, my son,
All will be well when the day is done.

Day is done, day is done.

When the day is done, when the day is done.

Tell me why you're smiling, my son.

Is there a secret you
can tell everyone?

Do you know more
than those that are wise?

Can you see what we all disguise
through your loving eyes?

And if you take my hand, my son,
All will be well when the day is done.

And if you take my hand, my son,
All will be well when the day is done.

Day is done,
when the day is done.
When the day is done,
when the day is done.

AFTERWORD

CHILDREN'S WISDOM AND GOODNESS OF SPIRIT is a powerful force that can inspire us and renew us when, as adults, our hearts become weary or confused. Children can light the path of healing if only we will let them take our hand and lead us when we have lost our way. "Day Is Done" expresses my belief that the inherent goodness we possess as small children is a precious gift that we must nurture, care for, and sustain as long as possible. If our early acceptance of one another, our pleasure in making and being friends, our intuitive lack of fear and mistrust, and our heartfelt embrace of one another can continue in our adult lives, it can provide the key to unraveling the root causes of the many challenges and conflicts that surround us.

My songs, such as "Day Is Done," were inspired by music created, mostly anonymously, by honest, real folks who, I believe, had somehow retained the wonderment of that childlike spirit within them. Theirs are the traditional songs that have lasted, and that first inspired me as a child. These songs told me their stories of pain and joy, glory and loss—their unvarnished, uncompromised truths. Such songs are waiting to teach you and your children the small and great lessons that helped me, and still help me, find my way. For this I will be forever grateful.

—Peter Yarrow

STERLING and the distinctive Sterling logo are registered
trademarks of Sterling Publishing Co., Inc.

Library of Congress Cataloging-in-Publication Data Available

4 6 8 10 9 7 5
10/09
Published by Sterling Publishing Co., Inc.
387 Park Avenue South, New York, NY 10016
Text © 2009 by Peter Yarrow
Illustrations © 2009 by Melissa Sweet
Distributed in Canada by Sterling Publishing
c/o Canadian Manda Group, 165 Dufferin Street
Toronto, Ontario, Canada M6K 3H6
Distributed in the United Kingdom by GMC Distribution Services
Castle Place, 166 High Street, Lewes, East Sussex, England BN7 1XU
Distributed in Australia by Capricorn Link (Australia) Pty. Ltd.
P.O. Box 704, Windsor, NSW 2756, Australia

Printed in China
All rights reserved.

Sterling ISBN 978-1-4027-4806-6

For information about custom editions, special sales, premium and
corporate purchases, please contact Sterling Special Sales
Department at 800-805-5489 or specialsales@sterlingpublishing.com.

The text was set in Worcester and Chikita.
The artwork was done in watercolor and mixed media.
Designed by Judythe Sieck and Chrissy Kwasnik.

Dedicated to my beloved brother, Andy,
for whom I wrote *Day Is Done* — P. Y.

To all the new little ones in our family,
Ellie, North, Liam, Sasha, and Haley,
and their parents — M. S.

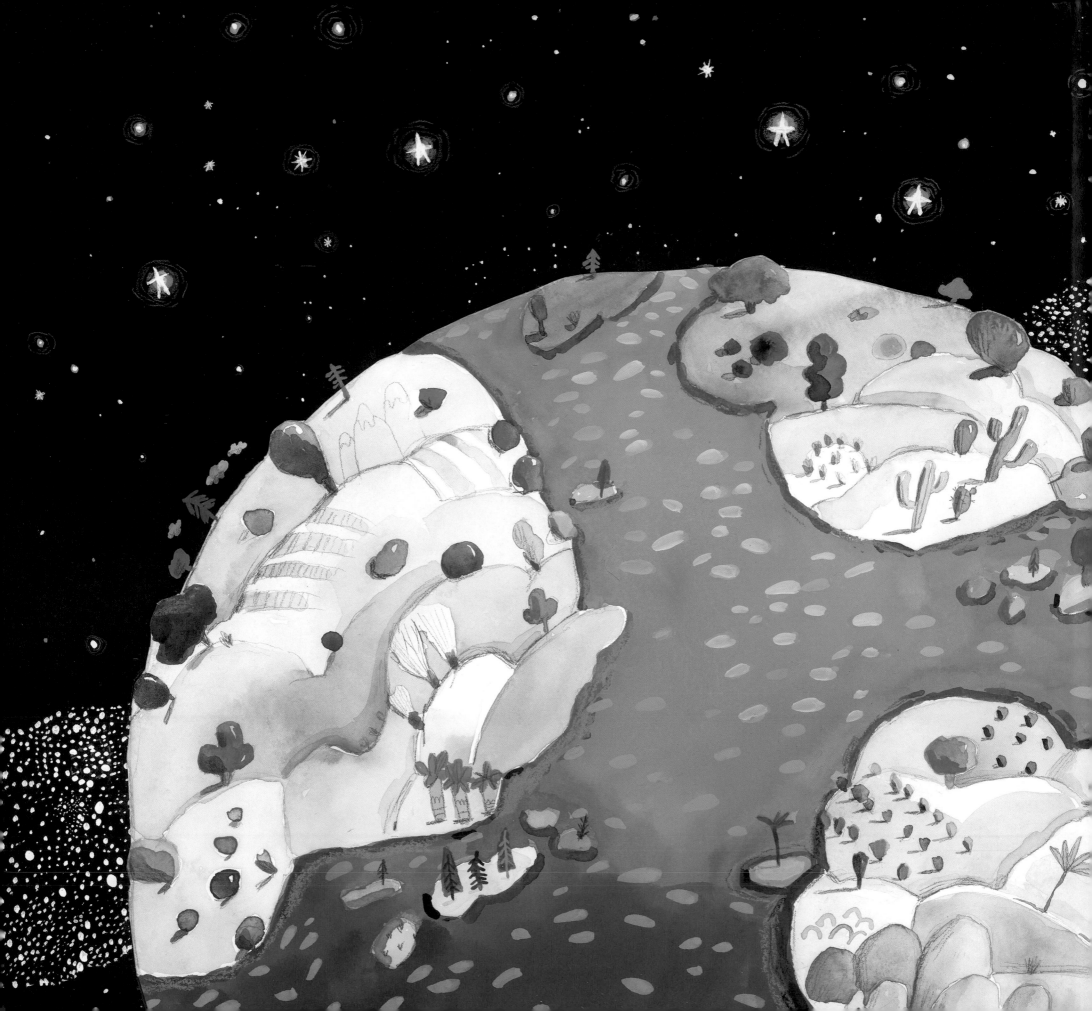